FLYING CARROTS

Written by S. A. Cornell
Illustrated by John Jones

Troll Associates

Library of Congress Cataloging in Publication Data

Cornell, S.A.
   Flying carrots.

   Summary: Farmer Rabbit explains his ambitious plans
for the flying carrots he is planting.
   [1. Carrots—Fiction. 2. Rabbits—Fiction.
3. Stories in rhyme] I. Jones, John, 1935-   ill.
II. Title.
PZ8.3.C185Fl   1986   [E]   85-14093
ISBN 0-8167-0640-9 (lib. bdg.)
ISBN 0-8167-0641-7 (pbk.)

FLYING CARROTS

My good friend Farmer Rabbit
grows tasty things each year.
His corn and beans and turnips
are famous far and near.

So when I stopped to ask him,
"What will you plant today?"
I really did not think at all
that this is what he'd say:

"My friend, this year is special.
I have big plans, you see.
For I'll plant flying carrots
that will come on home to me.

"These carrots will be big and
     orange,
just like the ones we love.
Except they won't stay in the
     ground.
They'll fly a bit above.

"And when it's time to pick them,
I won't get on my knees.
I'll just give a little whistle.
And they'll fly home on the breeze.

"Perhaps you'd like to stay a while, and help me plant these seeds. There's work enough for two to do. Just look at all these weeds!

13

"If you will stay and work with me
until it's time for lunch,
when carrots fly—about July—
I'll send you a big bunch."

I listened very closely
till I couldn't stand it longer.
Then I just had to say to him,
"My friend, you couldn't be
wronger.

"No! Carrots do not do these
     things.
They do not…will not try.
The carrots I have always seen
do not know how to fly!

"You may know how to grow
      great peas.
Your corn grows very high.
But please give up this new idea.
No! Carrots DO NOT fly."

Now Rabbit smiled and
    laughed a bit
and pulled seeds from his jacket.
"These plants WILL fly. I'm
    sure of it.
It says so on the packet.

"It's just that you have never tried.
Please don't give up just yet.
These carrots WILL fly home to us,
just like those speedy jets.

"Perhaps they'll grow to six feet
        long.
They'll hold us quite well then.
We'll sit and talk on carrot stalks
and fly around till ten.

"We'll have a very jolly time.
We'll fly. We'll glide. We'll speed.
We'll show them off to all our friends.
We will! We will, indeed!

"Yes, everyone who sees us fly
will want to come along.
We'll build in seats. We'll serve
     friends treats.
I know we can't go wrong."

I listened, but could not believe
all that my friend told me.
I had to tell him right away
that I did not agree.

"No, carrots do not do these
        things.
They do not…will not try.
The carrots I have always seen
do not know how to fly.

"You may know how to plant
      straight rows.
Your seedlings never die.
But please forget this silly plan.
No! Carrots DO NOT fly!"

But now it was too late to stop.
Farmer Rabbit was too busy.
He dreamed about his carrot jets
and looked so very dizzy.

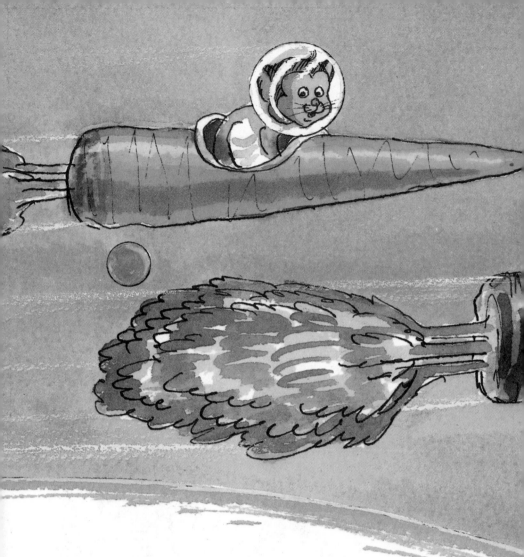

"We'll fly around the world,"
  he said.
"And aim out to a star.
We'll put our silver space suits on.
We'll drive our carrots far.

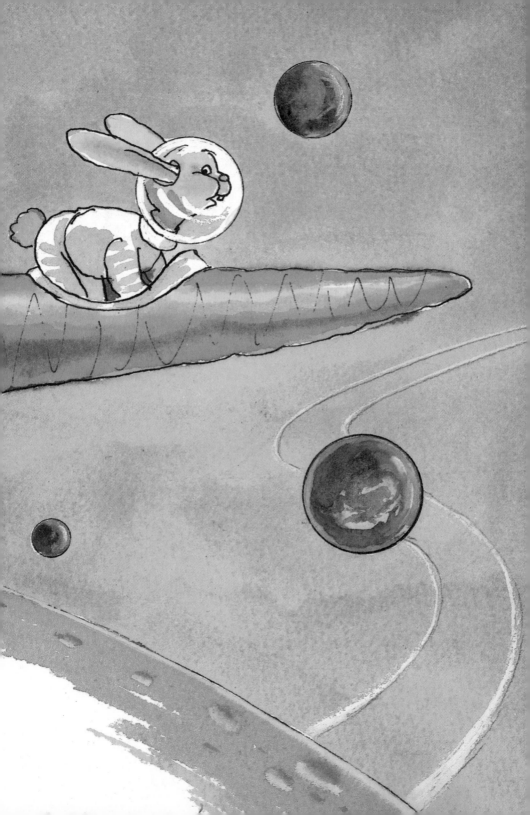

"You'll lead our carrot ships out
     there.
You really are a winner.
You'll find a happy spot for us
to land and then have dinner.

35

"We'll eat a bit of carrot.
Then we'll look both low and high
to find a place to plant more seeds
of carrots that can fly."

36

"Now wait," I finally yelled to
      him.
"This really must stop here.
Your dream must end. I say
      again.
It's gone too far I fear.
No! Carrots do not do these
      things.
They do not…will not try.
The carrots I have always seen
do not know how to fly.

"Your dreams are great. Believe
    me, friend.
You know I do not lie.
But please give up. It will not
    work.
No. Carrots DO NOT fly."

He looked at me. And then he spoke.
He cried a little tear.
"If you don't TRY to do great things,
you won't go far, my dear."

I looked at him. I nearly cried.
What he had said was true.
Just 'cause I'd never seen them fly,
doesn't mean they never do.

I said to him, "Yes, friend,
    you're right.
I'll let you be my guide.
You never know. We must
    have dreams.
Flying carrots we MAY ride!"

And so we worked together
planting seeds into the ground.
We weeded, raked, and shoveled
until lunch time rolled around.

Now all the seeds are in the earth.
So far no carrots grow.
But come July, perhaps we'll fly.
I'll surely let you know!